Churchill's TALE of TAILS

Anca Sandu

PEACHTREE
ATLANTA

Published by
PEACHTREE PUBLISHERS
1700 Chattahoochee Avenue
Atlanta, Georgia 30318-2112
www.peachtree-online.com

Text and illustrations © 2012 by Anca Sandu

First published in Great Britain in 2012 by Jonathan Cape,
an imprint of Random House Children's Publishers UK
First United States version published in 2014 by Peachtree Publishers

The illustrations were rendered in Adobe Illustrator by combining digital color
with hand-drawn textures and shading.

Cataloging-in-Publication Data
is available from the Library of Congress
ISBN 978-1-56145-738-0 / 1-56145-738-8
Printed in November 2013 in China
10 9 8 7 6 5 4 3 2 1
First Edition

To Joe, Sue, and Abi
for believing in me
—A. S.

Churchill was a very proud pig,
just like any other pig.

This is his

TALE *of* **TAILS**.

Churchill valued many things in life:

smelling beautiful flowers,

painting self-portraits,

playing classical music,

and reading good books.

And he loved to have tea
with his friends Billy and Gruff.

But Churchill had one
thing that he prized above
everything else...

his tail.

It wasn't a big tail.

It wasn't a fancy tail.

It wasn't even a very practical tail.
But it was his tail,

and it made
him feel great.

But one morning...

his tail was nowhere to be found.

Churchill searched here,

there,

and everywhere.

Finally, he gave up searching.
He was miserable.

"I just don't feel like myself
without my tail," he said.

Billy and Gruff
came up with
a good idea.

They gave Zebra a call.

The zebras were happy to help.
They had a spare tail
for Churchill to try.

But the zebra tail didn't feel quite right.

Perhaps I should try some other tails, Churchill thought.

So he went to see Peacock.

Peacock gave Churchill a tail that made him feel beautiful.
"Ooh," said Churchill to himself. "I wonder what other tails I could try."

A tail from the fish made Churchill feel fantastic!
He could do things he'd never done before.

Churchill never talks to us anymore. It's all these fancy tails.

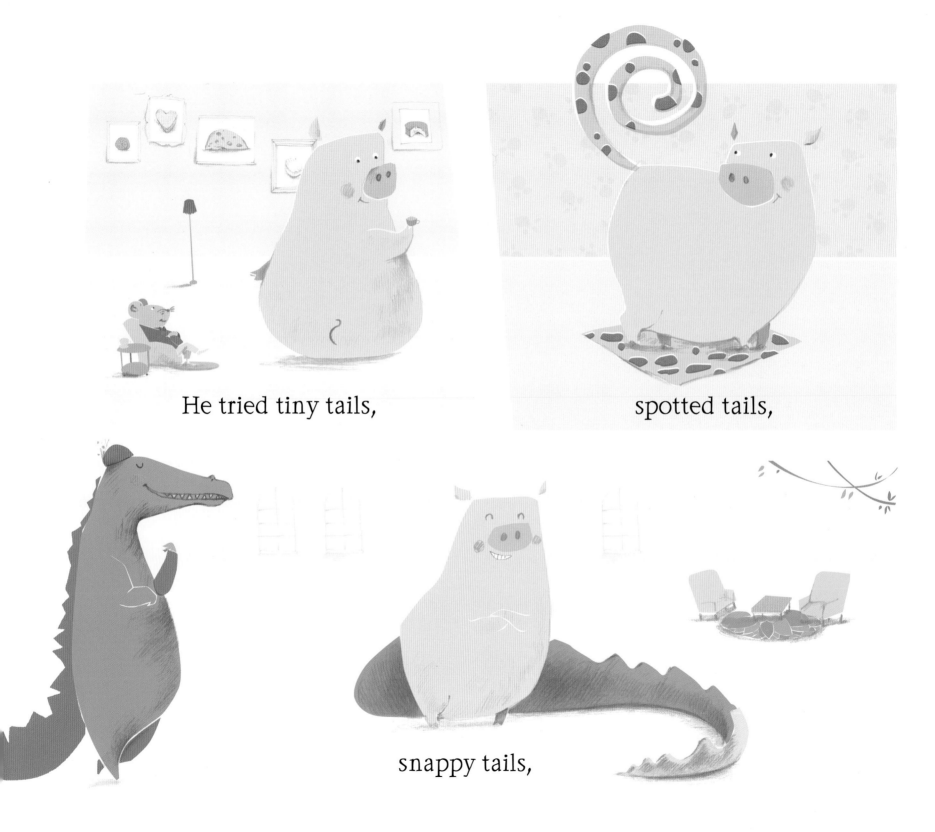

He tried tiny tails,

spotted tails,

snappy tails,

and tails that made him feel **big.**

Trying different tails made Churchill feel so good
that he didn't have time for anything else—

Come and play,
Churchill.

not even his old friends.

No, thank you,
I'm rather busy with
my new tails.

Now, thought Churchill,
    it's time for something very special.

So he went to Tiger's house.

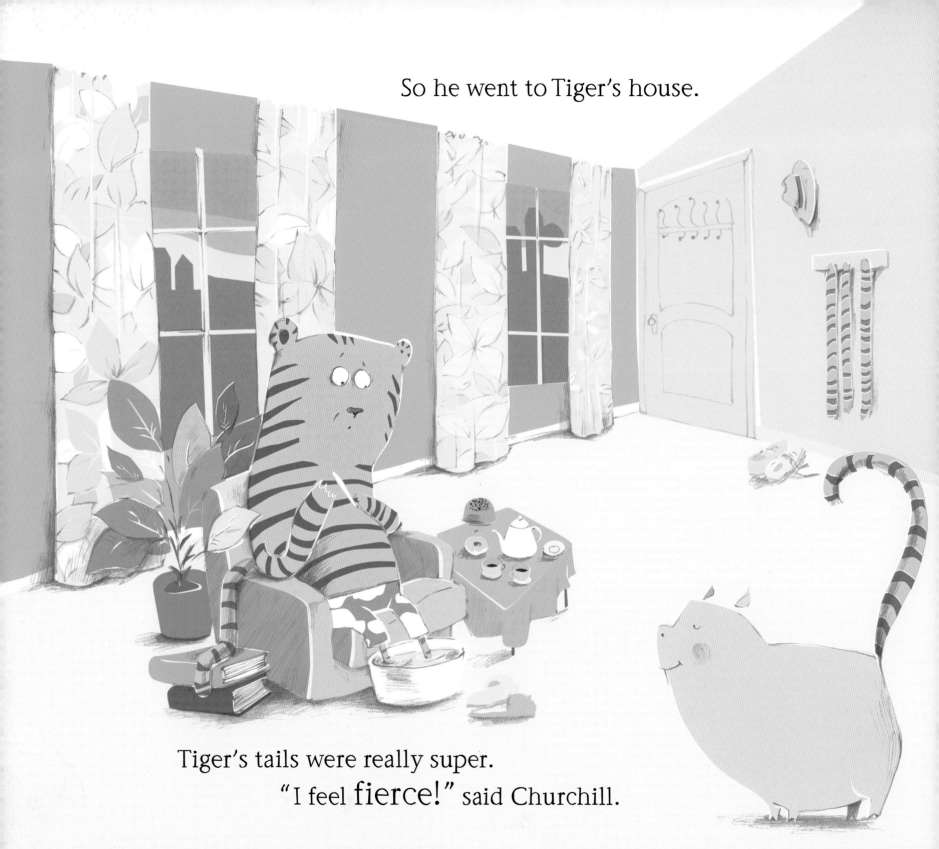

Tiger's tails were really super.
"I feel fierce!" said Churchill.

"I am the world's strongest, bravest pig," he said.

"I'm not scared of anything! I'm totally fearless!" But then...

a dark shadow
fell across his path.

Eeek!

Churchill felt terrified and very alone.

What could it be?

A giant mean lizard?

An unfriendly blue alien?

Or a huge hungry robot
with a twisted fork on its head?

But it wasn't any of those things.
It was just a little bird.

"What's that on your head?"
asked Churchill. "Is it my tail?"

"Well, I don't know," the bird replied. "I found it in a bush.

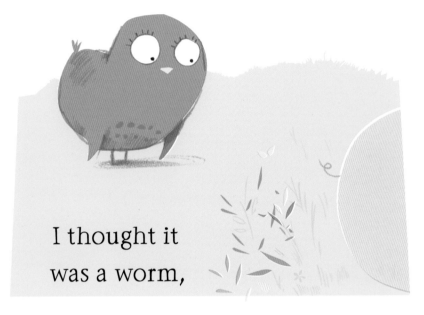

I thought it was a worm,

but I couldn't eat it.

It didn't look like a flower.

It was useless. So I put it on my head. I've grown rather fond of it."

"Oh, but it is my
very own perfect tail,"
said Churchill.
"Please may I have
it back?"

"Well," said Bird, "if it's yours then you should have it!"
"Thank you," said Churchill.

Finding his old tail made Churchill
feel like his old self again.
He was so grateful that he
helped Bird find the perfect
thing for her head.

And making a kind new friend
helped Churchill remember his old ones.

So he organized a tea party to bring all his friends together. "My dear friends," said Churchill, "I have been a very silly pig, and a very bad friend. Can you ever forgive me?"

And they did, because they loved Churchill
(even though he could be very silly).
From then on, Churchill took great care
of his own perfect tail,

and he was perfectly happy with it...

most of the time.